Now What?

Now What?

Sylvia Villasenor

XULON PRESS

Xulon Press
2301 Lucien Way #415
Maitland, FL 32751
407.339.4217
www.xulonpress.com

Printed in the United States of America.

Paperback ISBN-13: 978-1-66281-276-7
Hardcover ISBN-13: 978-1-66281-277-4
Ebook ISBN-13: 978-1-66281-278-1

Here is my family. I am the newborn baby girl Dad is holding. Dad, Mom, and I just arrived home from the hospital, and I am being introduced to my brother and five sisters. We are a total of seven children, six girls and one boy. Girls rule in this house.

n the months to come, Mom was going to be busy with the house chores and seven children. Grandma Ruth, my dad's mom, came from far away to stay with us for six months to help Mom with the house chores and the children. What a blessing for Mom and Dad.Grandma woke up early every morning to help my older sisters get ready for school. She dressed them, fed them breakfast, and made their school lunches. This allowed Mom to catch up on her sleep because I kept her up at night. Grandma also walked the girls to school, and a neighbor would pick them up after school and bring them home.

My three-, almost four-year-old brother and my one-and-a-half-year-old sister did not attend school yet, so they were home during the day when my older sisters were at school.

9

Every day was a busy day for Mom and Grandma. When they were done with the house chores, Mom would take a nap while I slept.

Grandma would get an early start with dinner to allow herself some free time when the older girls came home from school. As soon as the girls got home, they changed into their play clothes and ran out to the backyard to have some playtime with my brother and sister that were not in school yet. After play time, Grandma went outside to be with the children. She sat on a stool and the children sat around her, because she loved to tell them stories. She did this to calm them down so they could focus on homework after. By the time Dad came home, playtime and homework were out of the way. This allowed Dad to enjoy a peaceful dinner and evening.

One Saturday morning, when I was four months old, Mom woke up with a strong pain on the right side of her tummy. She told Dad and Grandma that she was not feeling well, and that the pain on the side of her tummy was making her dizzy and very tired. Dad told her to go back to bed and rest. Maybe she had hurt her side picking up one of the younger children and she needed to lay down. Dad assured Mom that he and Grandma would take care of the children and the house chores while she rested.

Mom went back to bed, and a few of the children ran inside her bedroom to be with her. Dad constantly checked on Mom while she rested, and to make sure the children that were in the bedroom with her were not making too much noise.

13

Not too long after the children left Mom's bedroom, Dad came in to check on her, and she began to break into a cold sweat with chills. She started to throw up. This did not seem normal to Dad. He got worried and decided to rush Mom to the hospital.

When they arrived at the hospital, Dad rushed to the front desk to check Mom in. When the nurse saw how sick Mom was, Mom was quickly put in a room and had the doctor come in to see her right away. After the doctor finished checking Mom, he became overly concerned. Mom had a ruptured appendix that was not caught in time and damaged other organs inside her body, as well as her blood. It was too late to fix the damaged organs. Mom was not going to make it; she had less than three days to live.Mom and Dad were in shock and very confused. This was hard to understand. "What is next?" they asked the doctor. The doctor was also in shock. All he could tell them was that he was going to transfer Mom to a private patient room. There she would be given pain medicine so she could be comfortable with no pain.

15

Mom was transferred to a private patient room and Dad stayed by her side.

After a few hours, Mom asked Dad to go home to talk to Grandma Ruth about what was to come, and to also contact her mother, sister, and brother who lived far away. She asked Dad to come back as soon as possible and bring the three older girls. At the time, the ages of my three older sisters were twelve, ten, and eight. Mom wanted to personally talk to them to let them know what was to come.

Dad went home and followed Mom's instructions, spoke to Grandma, and went right back to the hospital with the three older girls. When Dad arrived with the girls, the doctor was by Mom's bedside. Dad sat by Mom's bed with the girls until the doctor left the room.

Mom called the girls over to talk to them. As she held them close, she told them that her body was sick, too sick to continue living. She then reassured them that this was God's plan and Mom would be okay. God was soon going to send His angels to take her to heaven. Then God was going to make Mom our guardian angel that would always watch over us. The last things she told the girls were to take care of each other and help Dad with the house chores and the two youngest baby sisters. She made Dad promise her to always keep us together, and never separate us and send us to live with people we did not know well. The children must always stay together; that was her last request.

Dad agreed to follow Mom's request, and the three older girls did also. When the hospital visitation hours were over, they kissed Mom goodbye with the hope that they would be back to see her the following day.

When Dad and the girls arrived home from the hospital, Grandma gave Dad the news that she called Mom's mother, brother, and sister to notify them of Mom's unexpected illness. They were all in shock and felt helpless that they were not able to take a three-hour flight to be by Mom's side. Dad and Grandma felt hopeless; all they could do was pray for strength. Dad and Grandma stayed up late that night. The following morning, Mom's doctor called Dad to notify him that Mom had died peacefully.

This day was the hardest day for Dad, Grandma, and my three older sisters who were old enough to understand what had happened to Mom. Dad notified our family members that lived nearby, their close friends, and the neighbors. Grandma made a long-distance telephone call to notify the family members that lived far away.

Dad got his strength that day to arrange funeral services, with help from close family members that came to our home right away to help.

At the end of the day, Grandma stayed with all of us in the bedroom. She put everyone to bed and did not leave our sight all night.

Mom's memorial service was held a week after she died. After the service, friends and family came to our home with food, drinks, and sweets. Everyone sat around the dining room table to eat and talk about Mom. They celebrated her life by saying wonderful things about her. Mom was a soft-spoken, gentle soul who touched lives in a kind manner.

Many friends of Mom and Dad, including our neighbors, asked Dad if they could be of any help to him. They offered to buy groceries, drive the older children to school, and babysit. A few close friends asked Dad if he was open to adopting any of us. Dad had a hard time understanding why family friends would consider it, since it would be breaking the family apart. Dad kindly thanked them all for being so considerate and quickly expressed to them that my Mom's wish and last request was to keep the children together. Dad had to do whatever it took to keep us together, and preferably surrounded by immediate family members.

A few days after the memorial service, the family was getting ready for dinner. Grandma Ruth was sitting at the dinner table with four of my sisters. Dad was trying to get me to fall asleep, so he could eat dinner. My brother and sister were standing next to Dad, waiting for him to sit down at the dinner table.

Grandma was talking to Dad; she was telling him that soon she would be going back home. Grandma then asked Dad what his plans were regarding childcare. Dad's response was, "Mother, I do not know. Childcare costs for seven children will run me a fortune. What can I do, Mother?" he asked.Grandma Ruth told Dad that she had spoken to my mom's mother by phone. They both had a conversation, and they wanted to ask Dad if he would be open to the children moving to our grandmothers' hometown to live with them. This town was far away, three hours by airplane and two days by bus or train. They both lived close to each other; it was about a three-minute walk. This would make it easy for both grandmothers to manage taking care of us and the cost to have us all there for Dad would be less expensive. Financially, Dad would be able to manage. This town was the same town Mom and Dad grew up in. We also had many close relatives that lived there.

Dad was in shock when Grandma Ruth proposed this to him. His response was, "How can I give up on my children, allowing them to move so far away, after losing my wife?" He cried to Grandma, but he did not rule it out completely and asked Grandma to allow him time to think it over for a few days. Grandma told Dad to take his time and weigh the good and the bad reasons to agree to this solution for the benefit of the children.

A few weeks went by, and Dad was now ready to discuss this issue with Grandma. He had plenty of sleepless nights in deep prayer for a wise decision. Dad spoke to Grandma one on one, and he agreed to allow us to move away with both our grandmothers. Mom and Dad each had a sister that was not married and still living at home with each one of the grandmothers. These two aunts would be of great help to us. They both had jobs but would be there for us once they got home from work.

Shortly after this was agreed upon, the day came for us to make the big move. Dad drove us and Grandma to the airport to fly to our new home. This new place would be our new home for an indefinite amount of time. For Dad, it was another emotionally hard day. It was going to be hard for him, being alone, but he was going to have to manage. Thank God he had close family members and friends to help him cope.

Dad reassured everyone that once we arrived at our destination, our mom's family and his family would be at the airport waiting for us to arrive and drive us to our new home. They all said their final goodbyes to Dad, and we boarded the plane to begin our three-hour journey.

Once we arrived at our destination, my sisters, brother, and Grandma were so excited to get off the airplane. It had been a long flight for everyone.

Outside in the waiting area, to my Grandma Ruth and sisters' surprise, a group of family members were outside waiting to greet us. They were holding welcome signs; it was just as Dad said. Our grandma, aunts, uncles, and cousins were there with big smiles and hugs. My sisters were so happy with this warm welcome; so was Grandma Ruth. She was also happy and relieved we arrived safe.

For the next five years, this new place would become our home. Dad came to visit at least four times a year. We all fell in love with the town, our family members, and the town residents. They fell in love with us also. We were well taken care of, loved, and lacked nothing. It was a healthy environment for children to grow in.

Surely, God's hand was in all the chain of events that transpired since Mom's death, even in the future days to come, along with new changes. God's hand was always there to guide and clear the path that eventually reunited us with Dad after five years of living apart.

The End

CPSIA information can be obtained
at www.ICGtesting.com
Printed in the USA
BVHW020854311022
650736BV00007B/227